NOW YOU CAN READ...

The Little Mermaid

STORY ADAPTED BY LUCY KINCAID

ILLUSTRATED BY ERIC KINCAID

BRIMAX BOOKS · NEWMARKET · ENGLAND

The King of the Sea and his family
live in a palace on the seabed.
Fish swim in and out of the palace
all the time. The King's family
have tails like the fish.

The King's daughters
are the mermaids.
They find things
from shipwrecks.
They put them
in their gardens.
One little mermaid
has a statue of
a boy in her
garden.

Her grandmother
tells her stories.
The little mermaid
likes stories
about people.

When mermaids grow up they can go to the surface of the sea. This is the first time the little mermaid has been to the surface. The sea is shiny and flat, like glass. She can see a ship.

There is a prince on the ship. He is like the statue of the boy in her garden.

The wind begins to blow. There is
a storm coming. It starts to rain.
The ship is tossed by the waves.
Suddenly the ship turns over. It
is sinking. The prince is thrown
into the water. He is drowning.

The little mermaid does not want the prince to drown. She puts her arms round him. She stops him sinking. The waves take them to the shore. The little mermaid lays the prince on the sand. His eyes are closed but he is alive.

There is someone
coming. The little
mermaid hides
behind a rock. She
sees some girls.
The girls see the prince. They do
not see the little mermaid. They
carry the prince away.

The little mermaid
goes home to the
palace under the
sea. She sits in
her garden and
looks at the
statue of the boy.
She thinks about
the prince all
the time.

Her mermaid sisters find out where
the prince is living. They take the
little mermaid to the place.

The little mermaid
visits the bay
every night. She
watches the prince.
She cannot go
to him because
she cannot walk.
She has no feet.
Every night she is
more sad. "I will
ask the witch to
change my tail
into legs and
feet," she says.
"Then perhaps
the prince will
love me."

"I will help if you give me your voice," says the witch. The little mermaid loves to sing but she loves the prince more. "You will die if the prince ever loves another better than you!" warns the witch.

"Please do as
I ask," says the
little mermaid.
The witch mixes
her a potion.

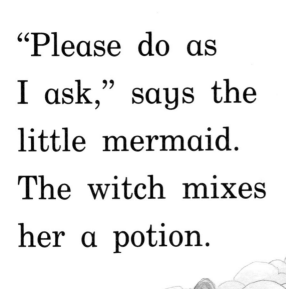

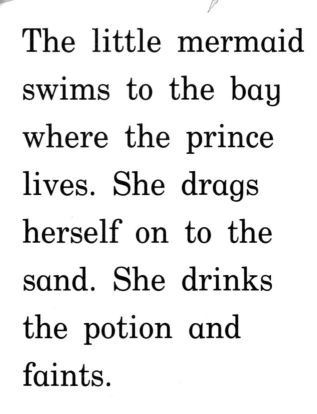

The little mermaid
swims to the bay
where the prince
lives. She drags
herself on to the
sand. She drinks
the potion and
faints.

When the little mermaid opens her eyes, the prince is standing beside her. "Who are you?" he asks. "Where have you come from?" She cannot answer because she has no voice.

The prince takes her to his palace. Her new feet hurt with every step she takes.

The little mermaid dances gracefully. Nobody knows how much her new feet hurt.

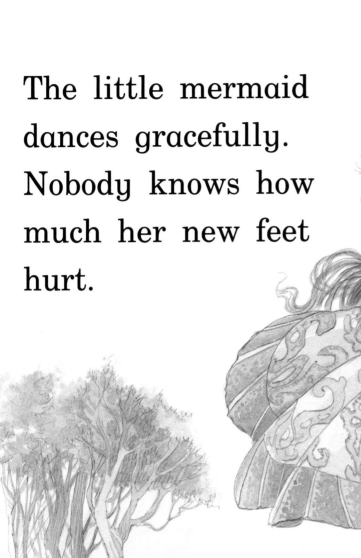

When the prince goes riding, he takes the little mermaid with him. At night she sleeps on a velvet cushion outside his door.

One night, when everyone is asleep, she goes to bathe her feet in the sea. Her sisters come to see her. They tell her they miss her. Her father and her grandmother are missing her too. They wave to her from some way off.

The prince grows to
love the little
mermaid like a
sister. She is
very happy. Then,
one day, the King
sends the prince
to see a princess.
The prince does not
want to go. The
King says he must.

As soon as the prince sees the princess he wants to marry her. The little mermaid remembers what the witch said. She is very sad. She knows she will die. On the day of the wedding everyone is happy, except for the little mermaid.

After the wedding they go on board
a ship. The little mermaid's sisters
follow the ship. They have cut off
their long hair. "We have found
a way to save you," they call
to the little mermaid. "We have
given the witch our hair. In return
she has given us a knife which
will break the spell."

Then the sisters shout to the little mermaid, "You must kill the prince. His blood must fall on your feet. Then your feet will turn back into a tail. You will be a mermaid again and you can come back to our palace under the sea."

The little mermaid looks at the sleeping prince. She cannot harm him. She would rather die herself. The little mermaid throws the knife into the sea. Then she throws herself into the sea. She changes into sparkling foam and is never seen again.

All these appear in the pages of
the story. Can you find them?

King of the Sea

mermaid

statue

ship